199

THE OGOPOGO AFFAIR

THE OGOPOGO AFFAIR

Mel D. Ames

*With a comprehensive update
of the legendary monster,
OGOPOGO*

Mosaic Press
Oakville-New York-London

CANADIAN CATALOGUING IN PUBLICATION DATA

Ames, Mel D., 1921-
The Ogopogo affair

ISBN 0-88962-538-7

1. Ogopogo. I. Title
QL89.2.O34A64 1992   001.9'44   C93-093064-9

Published by MOSAIC PRESS, P.O. Box 1032, Oakville, Ontario, L6J 5E9, Canada. Offices and warehouse at 1252 Speers Road, Units #1&2, Oakville, Ontario, L6L 5N9, Canada.

Mosaic Press acknowledges the assistance of the Canada Council and the Ontario Arts Council in support of its publishing programme.

Copyright © Mel D. Ames, 1993
Design and cover illustration by Patty Gallinger
Typeset by Jackie Ernst

Printed and bound in Canada.

ISBN 0-88962-538-7 PB

MOSAIC PRESS:
In Canada:
     MOSAIC PRESS, 1252 Speers Road, Units 1&2, Oakville, Ontario L6L 5N9, Canada. P.O. Box 1032, Oakville, Ontario, L6J 5E9.

In the U.K.:
     John Calder (Publishers) Ltd., 9-15 Neal Street, London, WCZH 9TU, England.

FOR KATHY

FOREWORD

THE OGOPOGO AFFAIR was first published in MIKE SHAYNE MYSTERY MAGAZINE in October, 1984. It is, *per se*, a murder mystery, centered in the Okanagan Valley and written around the legendary lake monster, Ogopogo, the existence of which was as controversial then as it is today.

Since that initial publication, Ogopogo (or *N'ha-a-itk,* as the native Indians knew it), has continued to be sought after by hordes of tourists and curiosity seekers. A number of accredited biologists, zoologists, and oceanographers have joined their ranks, with varied results. To this day, however, unconfirmed sightings, blurred photographs and controversial videotapes are all that has surfaced from thousands of hours of Ogopogo watching.

Still, the legend survives, stronger than ever. After reading THE OGOPOGO AFFAIR, you may arrive at some conclusions of your own. Does *N'ha-a-itk* really exist? Are the reported sightings genuine, or merely flights of the imagination? Could THE OGOPOGO AFFAIR really have happened? Only you can decide.

The Author

TABLE OF CONTENTS

THE OGOPOGO AFFAIR

Stuart Blaze steered the sleek black van into a parking slot in front of the Royal Canadian Mounted Police building in the old north-end district of Kelowna. They had driven all night to get to this small jewel of a city, nestled midway along the eastern shore of Okanagan Lake, in the heart of beautiful British Columbia. A glance at his watch told Blaze it was a few minutes shy of 6:30. He was right on time.

Even at so early an hour, through the van's tinted windshield, Blaze could feel the heat of the Okanagan sun as it rose to its summer's task of ripening fruit and tanning the tender skins of tourists. In late July, the bright cloudless blue sky was a fairly predictable phenomenon; Stu Blaze being there to witness it, however, was not. *A rather bizarre case*, the inspector had implied by long-distance telephone, *something about a lake monster killing off the tourists.* Blaze shrugged inwardly. Old John had finally flipped.

Before leaving the vehicle, he drew the curtain behind the cab and smiled down at the sleeping form of Connie Wells, girl-Friday and new, self-appointed travel companion. She was curled up on the built-in, let-down bunk, half in and half out of the covers, looking more like an innocent waif than the duty-toughened ex-policewoman she really was.

It had been a tiring trip over the Canadian Rockies. They had left Calgary late Monday evening with Connie driving, then, somewhere between the sleepy mountain towns of Golden and Revelstoke, she had given up the wheel to Blaze and crawled into the back for a little shut-eye. He decided to let her sleep herself out.

1

Blaze locked the door as he left the van, then made for the entrance to the squat Administration building. He was a big man, Stuart Blaze, six-four, with a thick bull-like neck and massive shoulders. His short-cut, wiry blonde hair glistened like a Brillo pad in the morning sun. He walked tall and proud, with a confidence that came of knowing precisely where he stood in a world of conflict between good and evil men. Twenty years on the Force will add that certain style and stature to a dedicated man.

A pretty receptionist looked up with a smile from behind the front counter. A small sign told Blaze her name was Jan Thurston, a civilian employee.

"Inspector Warfield is expecting me," he said to her, returning the smile.

"Oh, yes." The girl referred to an open date book. "You must be Sergeant Blaze."

"*Mr.* Blaze, now."

"Yes, well --- come right in, *Mr.* Blaze." Her smile broadened. She pressed a buzzer that released the automatic lock on the door to the inner offices, then pointed a dainty finger. "It's the first office on the left."

Blaze had barely stepped inside when a tall, gray-haired man with deeply chiselled features shoved his head out of an office doorway. "Stu! I thought I heard you come in. Damn it, man, it's been a long time."

The men shook hands warmly.

"You look as obscenely fit as ever, you old rascal." The inspector drew the big ex-Mountie into the office and closed the door. He motioned Blaze to a chair, then settled himself comfortably behind his desk. He was all smiles. "Your new career as a P.I. must agree with you," he said approvingly.

Blaze flushed with modest pride. "Thanks to referrals from the Force, John, it's been going well."

Inspector John Warfield made a steeple with his fingers, pursed his thin lips against it and squinted his pale gray eyes. "The grapevine has it that young Connie Wells, from the Calgary Detachment, took

2

her 'purchase' a few weeks ago, just so she could go to work full-time for you, Stu. That a fact?''

Blaze flushed a little deeper. He had been expecting this. At the time, he had been vehemently opposed to what he felt was an impetuous move by Connie to 'buy her way' out of the R.C.M.P. She had been one of the original Troop 17, of 1974, the first group of women ever to enter the Force. She had over nine years under her Sam Browne when she made the big decision to walk away from it all. It wasn't something that she, or he, had taken lightly. But it was done, and he didn't particularly want to talk about it now.

''Yeah, Connie's with me,'' he said quietly. ''It was her choice, John. She's of age.''

''No need to be defensive about it, Stu. Knowing you, you probably did your best to talk her out of it. I just wanted to get my facts straight. That's all.''

''Okay, John, so now you've got it straight.'' Blaze shifted uncomfortably in his chair. ''What have you got lined up for me this morning?'' he asked, eager to change the subject, ''You sounded desperate on the phone.''

''I *am* desperate, Stu. We've got ourselves a P.R. problem you wouldn't believe. I was sent in from Vancouver to try to get a handle on it. Ever hear of Ogopogo?''

''Ogo---who?''

''Ogopogo,'' the inspector said again. ''And it's a 'what', not a 'who' --- a legendary lake monster, is what it is, and a long-time inhabitant of Okanagan Lake.'' He leaned forward over his desk and his voice became quietly retrospective. ''A long snaky thing, Stu, over twenty feet long, they tell me, with, uh --- a horse or goat-like head ---''

Blaze seemed undecided whether to grin, groan, or keep looking serious. ''you're putting me on,'' he said finally.

John Warfield wasn't smiling. ''This is not a put-on, Stu. Ogopogo has long been a household word from one end of the Okanagan Valley to the other, and points far afield. There have been well over twenty recorded sightings, dating from as far back as 1852, involving scores of reliable eyewitnesses. Even prior to that, he (she) --- *it*, was well known to the local Indians as *N'Ha-a-itk*. According to legend, they, the Indians, used to throw sacrificial animals into the lake to appease the monster. Small pigs, chickens, things like that.''

Blaze cleared his throat. ''John, if you're about to tell me they're keeping Opo-gogo happy now by feeding it the odd tourist ---''

That's *Ogo-pogo*, Stu, not --- what you said. And stop trying to second-guess me. It isn't the tourists that are hurting, it's the tourist trade. Not to mention three dead Indians. Let me explain.''

''I wish you would.'' Blaze reached for a cigarette in a bid to curb his growing impatience. ''My business cards read P.I., John --- remember? --- not P.R.''

John Warfield drew his lips together in a thin white line. He leaned back in his swivel chair, his hands planted firmly on the desk. He was a striking man, even out of uniform. His age could have been anywhere between forty and sixty, in spite of the gray hair. ''Stu,'' he said with deadly calm, ''just shut up and listen, will you?''

Blaze shrugged his mountainous shoulders and drew heavily on the cigarette. ''It's your powwow,'' he said. A puff of blue smoke emerged from his mouth with each word.

Warfield, glaring, suddenly gave a reluctant chuckle. ''You look like you're sending up smoke signals,'' he said. His gray eyes glinted mischievously. ''I wonder if that isn't some kind of omen ---?''

''John, come *o-o-on*. All you're giving me is a lot of hocus-pocus. Lake monsters, Indian superstitions, pigs, chickens, smoke signals ---''

''You're forgetting three dead Indians.''

Blaze heaved a sigh. ''If only I could.''

The inspector got to his feet then and began to pace. ''Okay, okay. I was just giving you some background, Stu, because what I'm about to tell you is going to sound, well --- a little farfetched. All I ask is that you hear me out before you start jumping to conclusions.''

Blaze sent up three more signals. ''You got it,'' he said.

''Three weeks ago last Friday,'' Warfield began, ''an early morning jogger was crossing Okanagan Lake bridge when he stopped

4

to catch his breath and admire the view. Something in the water caught his eye. He'd heard about Ogopogo, of course, so he moved farther along the bridge to get a better look. When the thing in the water was directly beneath him, he recognized it as a human body, floating just below the surface ---''

"One dead Indian," Blaze speculated wryly.

"Right. It was a girl, Stu, mid teens. She was nude. At first, it was thought she had drowned, but the autopsy revealed otherwise."

"She'd been murdered?"

"She'd been *sacrificed*, Stu, crushed to death in the coils of the lake monster, Ogopogo."

Blaze groaned aloud. "John," he pleaded, "you've just got to be kidding."

The inspector leaned over his desk and yanked open the center drawer. He took out a brown manilla folder and plunked it down in front of Blaze. "I had Ghost put this together for you. It covers everything, from the moment the jogger discovered the body."

Ghost, Blaze knew, was Warfield's *aide-de-camp*, Sergeant Gary Goetze. He was known throughout the Force for his uncanny ability to eke out the most unlikely facts and figures on any*one* and any*thing*. The epithet was apt. Goetze had the soul of a computer and the gray physical deportment of a living ghost.

"I don't much like being taken for granted," Blaze grunted, "even by you and Ghost." He placed a restraining hand the size of a 20-oz T-bone on the unopened file. "And just why, may I ask, is this job being routed to me?"

John Warfield lowered himself back into his swivel chair. "Open the file," he said.

Blaze flipped back the brown cover and was visibly shaken. He found himself staring down at an enlarged colored glossy of a teen-aged Indian girl. She was sprawled, naked, over the rough planking of a lakeside wharf or pier, her once nubile body limp and lifeless, weirdly contorted. The bow of the police boat was fuzzy but discernible in the immediate background. The girl's eyes were open, wide with apparent horror, the mouth twisted in a silent scream.

The big ex-Mountie had seen death before. It was never pleasant. But what made this one unique, was a long purple bruise, the width of a man's arm, that circled the body in a continuous, unbroken spiral from the neck to the knees. It was as though a giant worm had wrapped itself around the girl --- and squeezed.

"Mother of God!" Blaze's gaze drifted incredulously from the girl to Warfield, then back to the girl. "I don't believe what I'm seeing."

"Then maybe you'll believe the next item in the file. It's the autopsy report."

Blaze turned the page.

"According to the Medical Examiner," Warfield told him as he read, "that girl was crushed, *literally crushed*; ribs snapped like matchsticks, shoulder and hip joints torn from their sockets, the pelvis split and crumbled --- it's all in there, Stu. But the most unnerving thing of all, as I see it, is that the internal havoc in that girl's body, is irrefutably consistent with the path of that long spiral bruise."

Blaze inhaled deeply as he browsed through the remaining file. "What other goodies have you got in here?"

"Two other girls. One about seventeen, one fourteen. Both Indians. They were found in the same general vicinity of the bridge, precisely a week apart. All three girls were pulled from the water nude, and to date, no trace of their clothing has been found. And, as you can see, they all had met the same grisly end."

"Were the girls molested?"

"Are you serious?"

"Sexually, I mean."

"No."

"Drugs?"

"All our tests have come up negative, Stu. We just don't know what to look for."

"No leads at all? Other than the Ogopogo thing?"

"None. But what other explanation could there possibly be? We're not only faced with an old Indian myth, remember; we're dealing here with hard medical evidence."

"How many people know about this?"

"We've managed to keep all three deaths under wraps, so to speak, until yesterday. Then the national Media got wind of them. The whole mess was aired on the News Hour, last night, so I guess Canada A.M. will be picking it up this morning. You got a TV built into that wheeled ark of yours?"

"Affirmative, but I doubt Canada A.M. will tell us anything that Ghost hasn't dug up already." Blaze levered himself out of his chair with a beleaguered sigh . He scooped up the file and headed for the door without a backward glance.

Warfield followed. "I knew I could count on you, Stu. Ghost will catch up with you later. He'll be your liaison with this office."

Blaze turned at the threshold. "I haven't yet said that I'd take the case, John. Let me give it some thought, kick it around with Connie ---" He shook his blond, bristly head. "I'll get back to you."

Warfield fought a knowing smile. He knew from past performance that once Stuart Blaze picked up a scent, he was the personification of Krazy Glue itself. In the true Mountie tradition, it had never been, and would not be now, a question of *would* he get his man (or, in this case, lake monster); it was merely a matter of *when*.

Blaze caught a whiff of freshly brewed coffee before he got to within ten feet of the van. The door opened for him magically as he approached, and as he ducked into the cab, he found himself on the receiving end of a morning kiss, amid the sensuous sounds and smells of sizzling bacon.

"Morning, boss." Connie Wells' smiling face glowed at him with the radiance of a morning sun. Her eyes had the color and sparkle of Creme-de-Menthe. She stood slim and trim in white cords and a matching shirt-blouse, a full foot shorter than his own seventy-six inches. Her abundant auburn hair, that she had decided to let grow after leaving the Force, still just barely brushed her collar. She put Blaze in mind of the bushy-tailed nymph in the Kellogg Special K commercials; the epitome of everything bright and beautiful.

"Morning, slave." He stifled a yawn. "I thought this domestic routine was strictly taboo in the new feminist manifesto."

She handed him a cup of coffee. ''I'm only a feminist when it pleases me,'' she said with a perverse, saccharine smile. ''One egg, or two?''

''Three.'' Blaze took a swallow of coffee and settled back comfortably on the leather settee-cum-bunk that ran down one side of the van. A small, open-up galley occupied the immediate corner and a color TV hung on a swivel from the headliner. Connie had already set a swingout table with breakfast accouterments.

''I don't feel good about this case,'' he told her as she flipped an egg. ''I'm used to hunting down criminals, not an overgrown worm with a head like a goat.''

Connie did a double-take. ''10-9, please.''

Blaze chuckled. She couldn't shake the habit of the R.C.M.P. codes. *10-9; repeat,please.* He reached up to the TV set.

''It's time for Canada A.M.,'' he said. ''They're supposed to have the whole story this morning. Suppose we listen to their version while we eat, then if there's anything they've missed, I'll fill you in later.''

''Whatever you say, lover.''

Blaze glanced at her with a look of mild concern. ''Fellow officer, I was,'' he told her quietly. ''Boss, I try to be. Dear and devoted friend, I truly am. But lover, Connie? That just hasn't happened.''

''Through no fault of mine,'' she said without embarrassment.

Blaze hunkered down against the leather cushions and loosed a long troubling sigh. ''I'm just not the guy for you, Connie. I'm in my forty-first year, remember? You don't want to mess around with a big old lug like me. You're still young, you're beautiful ---''

Connie turned her head and looked at him from atop a body that any teen-ager would have been proud of. ''I'm thirty-one, Stu, and that's no spring chicken. And the only time I feel really beautiful is when *you* look at me.'' She plunked a heaping plate of bacon and eggs on the table in front of him. ''You big jerk,'' she scowled, ''how'm I ever going to get you to say 'Uncle'?''

Blaze knew, of course, just as surely as she did, that he had already said 'Uncle' in his heart. She sat beside him with a smaller portion of the same breakfast, and he responded with charitable aplomb to a dig in the ribs for more elbow room. The final abdication of one's bachelorhood was not an easy thing for a man to accept, irrespective of the bribe.

Midmorning saw Blaze and Connie strolling out onto the mile-long, floating, Okanagan Lake bridge (the only one of its kind in Canada, they had just been told) to see at first hand the area where the bodies had surfaced. Their guide, a young constable who was obviously enjoying a respite from traffic duty, had been peripherally involved in all three recoveries.

"That's Hot Sands beach," he said, pointing back to where Kelowna's City Park met the lake edge, "the park is behind it, of course, and beyond that, the yacht club. You can see the masts of the sailboats poking up above the wharf. The girls' bodies were all spotted on this side of the bridge, the north side, between the lift span and the shoreline."

"Is there any current down there?" Blaze asked leaning over the rail.

"Current? This is a lake, Mr. Blaze, not a river, although it is almost a hundred miles long and no more than three miles across at any point. The entire valley is a veritable Mecca for tourists, especially during the summer months."

"Hot Sands beach is almost deserted," Connie noted in contradiction.

"Yes, mam." The constable chuckled grimly. "And it'll likely stay that way until someone snares the now infamous Ogopogo. Did you know there's a million dollars offered to anyone who catches the creature?"

"*A million dollars?*" Connie's vivid green eyes widened in amazement. "Who'd put up that kind of money?"

"The OSTA, I think. That's the Okanagan-Similkameen Tourist Association. Or was it the local Chamber of Commerce? Anyway, the million bucks has now been underwritten by Lloyds of London (can you believe it?), and was even mentioned in the House of

Commons, in Ottawa, by the local MP. See that building?'' The constable indicated a small, squat structure at the west end of the bridge. ''That's the Tourist INFO Center. They've apparently got some guy in there (a volunteer, I think) who's been pretty vocal about this whole thing. A retired fire chief, they tell me, by the name of Roland Rocque.''

''Roll and Rock?''

The young Mountie spelled it out. ''R-O-C-Q-U-E, pronounced rock, as in stone. His first name is Roland. He claims *N'Ha-a-itk* is on the warpath again.''

Blaze shrugged his shaggy eyebrows and turned his attention back to the shimmering surface of the lake. ''What has been the general public reaction to the drownings, constable?''

''Panic, what else? And they weren't drownings, Mr. Blaze.''

''Whatever.''

''Well --- most people seem to figure the girls must have been skinny-dipping off Hot Sands, and, I guess, that sometime during the night ---.''

''Alone? Skinny-dipping *alone*?''

The constable shrugged his epaulets. ''Who's to know, sir, what an Indian's going to do?''

Blaze winced inwardly. ''Then what became of their clothing?''

''Your guess is as good as mine, Mr. Blaze. Maybe their clothes were stolen. There are a lot of itinerant fruit pickers roaming the valley this time of year.''

''I understand all three bodies were found on a Friday morning, constable, subsequent Fridays.''

''Yes. And as near as the M.E. could tell, they'd been in the water anywhere between five to eight hours.''

Blaze stared off down the lake. ''They're in cahoots,'' he said absently, as much to himself as anyone.

''Who?'' Connie asked.

''The Indians and *N'Ha-a-itk*. They seem to be on the same timetable.''

"Maybe it's the grim aftermath of some kind of on-going Indian ritual," Connie said at his elbow.

"Maybe, maybe not." Blaze sighed heavily. "The more we get into this case, the curiouser it gets."

Connie echoed him, sigh and sound. "Curiouser and curiouser," she said.

Instead of following the causeway back to the city center, where the van was parked, Blaze and Connie left the constable at the east end of the bridge to amble down along the near deserted beach. Only two other pertinacious souls marred the long and otherwise empty expanse of sand. Blaze halted by a driftwood log that lay partially submerged, nudging the sandy shore. He hefted one end, then gave it a gentle shove with his toe.

"That could be a navigational hazard," Connie admonished as the log wallowed out into deeper water.

"So could Ogopogo," Blaze replied cryptically. "I guess it's just a question of priorities."

"I don't follow."

"According to the constable," Blaze reminded her, "those girls entered the water just about at this point, then floated around for five to eight hours until they were spotted --- *still* in this same general area. I'd like to see if the same thing happens to this log. You'll notice that it's roughly the same size and weight as the victims."

"Hmmm. That bloodhound brain of yours never quits. And here I thought you were just quietly enjoying our little stroll."

Blaze turned to smile at her. "I am," he assured her, but his eyes looked as fathomless as the lake.

They cut through the park then, skirting the busy sports oval and the tennis courts, lured on through the trees by the distant glimpse of a gala-looking old paddle-wheeler. It was the *Fintry Queen*, moored near the park's north entrance, where it vied for tourist attention with a billowing sculptured fountain, entitled 'Sails', and a twenty-foot mock-up of a horse-headed, spiny-backed, green-and-yellow replica of Ogopogo.

They paused there, to sit on the concrete lip of the fountain, where they could quietly ponder the malevolent creature that was terrorizing this small interior city. As they watched, a bikini-clad, blonde, teen-age girl began to pose for a camera-toting cohort. With one shapely young thigh wedged into the monster's gaping jaw, she contorted her sweet young face into a grim, comical mask of mock horror.

Connie chuckled nervously. "Not everyone, it seems, is fraught with fear."

"Would you be, at that age?"

Before Connie could respond, a man seemed suddenly to materialize in front of her, as though from nowhere. He moved soundlessly to her side and settled down, uninvited, like a puff of gray morning mist.

"Hi, Ghost," Blaze and Connie said in unison.

"Stu. Connie. You both look great."

Sergeant Gary Goetze had a voice that was as gray and weightless as his appearance. His face and his hands were the color of cigarette ash, his thinning hair a diluted, pallid grizzle. You had to get close to him to make out the faint, dusty curve of his eyebrows, and the eyes that peered hauntingly out from under them were the same smoky, ethereal gray as the rest of him. Even the plain-clothes he wore were nondescript and colorless. The nickname, Ghost, suited him well.

"You look great, too." Blaze heard Connie say, knowing she couldn't possibly be serious.

"Feel fine," Ghost said, "but I don't care much for this infernal Okanagan weather. It's been up in the mid-nineties for over a week now. I'm talking Fahrenheit, you understand. You can convert it to Celsius yourself, if that's your bag. I'm too damn old to change."

Blaze laughed. The current controversy over the Federal government's unpopular conversion to metric was rampant, especially in the west. "What have you got for me, Ghost? Any update on the file?"

"That file doesn't need an update, Stu, it needs a match. Have you ever run into anything so weird?"

"Never."

"Any ideas on how they died?"

"You're not buying the Ogopogo theory?"

Ghost treated them to a sinister grimace that Connie was sure had begun with every good intention of becoming a smile. "What do I know? I still believe in Rin-tin-tin." He reached into an inner pocket of his jacket and extracted a garish, multicolored handbill. "The circus is in town," he told them in his bland monotone. "It's pegged out on the main drag, Harvey Street, in that open field between Spall Plaza and Orchard Park shopping center. You might just be interested."

"In a circus?"

"They usually only set up a few rides for the kids," Ghost persisted, "and stay over for two or three days, but this time they've got a bit of a midway and a couple of sideshows. One of the latter is run by a guy by the name of Kurt Meyerbaum. He's been dragging them in for over three weeks now, with an endearing little critter he calls Cedric."

"So?"

Connie cringed as Ghost leaned across in front of her to confide in a tooth-baring, Bela Lugosi whisper against his palm, "Cedric is a twenty-two foot python."

Blaze narrowed his eyes at the grinning Ghost across the brink of Connie's startled profile. "That's a pig in a poke if I ever heard one," he snarled.

"Who said anything about a pig? I *said* ---"

"I know what you said," Blaze muttered, "and it's just too damn convenient to have the slightest relevance. I suppose this guy Meyerbaum also hates Indians ---"

"You got it."

"And he takes Cedric for a swim every Thursday night after the last show ---"

Ghost rose to his feet like a column of gray smoke. "You got a phone in that home-away-from-home?"

Blaze drew a card from his lapel pocket. It read, simply: *PRIVATE INVESTIGATIONS, Stuart Blaze.* The radio-telephone call numbers were inscribed in the bottom right-hand corner. "If

13

we're not in," he said, "leave a message with Warfield. I'll get back to you."

Connie stood, then turned and stooped to retrieve her purse from beside the fountain. When she straightened a moment later, Ghost was gone.

"Where'd he go?" she said in mild awe.

Blaze, who had been momentarily distracted by the aesthetics of Connie's last maneuver, did a quick three-sixty.

"Sonofagun," he said with a grin. "He must work at that."

They heard the calliopean sounds of the circus from half a mile away. The whirling glitter of the rides came into view next, and the smell of French fries and cotton candy assailed their nostrils before they had reached the turnstiles. It only remained then, to taste and touch, for all five senses to be blatantly seduced.

Blaze headed directly for the midway with Connie skipping along at his side, hanging onto his sleeve, taking two steps to his giant one.

"For something that isn't going to have the slightest relevance," she puffed, "you're sure in an unholy hurry to get to it."

Blaze's only response was a noncommittal grunt. But on reaching the crowded midway, he braked suddenly, and Connie piled into him with a startled "*Ooof!*" As she inspected her nose for damage, Blaze pointed triumphantly to an illuminated marquee that proclaimed in flashing, multi-colored lights: CEDRIC --- THE LARGEST REPTILE IN CAPTIVITY. And underneath, in more modest terms: *Handler, Kurt Meyerbaum.*

"I hate snakes," Connie asserted as she squeezed around a locked turnstile, hard on the heels of Blaze, then on through a door that ordered them with mute futility to KEEP OUT.

"Then you'd better watch where you step," Blaze cautioned, grinning as Connie groaned with new dismay.

Inside, Meyerbaum's canvas emporium was structured in the way of an old Shakespearean theatre, with encircling benches, converging down on a sunken central stage. The tent was dimly lit and empty, except for a huge glass enclosure that dominated the stage, and, hopefully, gave secure domicile to all twenty-two slithery feet of 'the largest reptile in captivity.'

As they neared the stage, they could make out the snake's indolent bulk, stretching from one end of its glass prison to the other, its scaly hide etched in diamond-like markings and imbued with earthy hues of brown, yellow, and muddy black. There was a subtle sense of movement to the inert body, an almost imperceptible inner pulse that seemed to ripple along its monstrous length and gather in a restless lump, a foot or two down from the flat leathery head.

"You know what that lump is?" Blaze asked with the unlikely innocence of an angler baiting a barbed hook.

Connie curled the end of her upper lip. "I'm not sure I want to know."

"That lump," said a deep voice from behind them, "is the still undigested remains of a doeling goat. Cedric, he favors pork, when he gets his druthers. Goats happen to be cheaper."

Blaze and Connie turned to face a tall, barrel-chested man with a head like an ostrich egg and an Adolph Menjou mustache that must have measured twelve inches across. He wore a black sleeveless T-shirt and matching leotards.

"Kurk Meyerbaum?"

"That's me. And you're from the police, right? I wondered when you'd get around to us."

Blaze identified himself, and Connie. "You were expecting us?"

"Of course. When three people die the way those Indians did, any boa constrictor in a fifty-mile radius has got to be a prime suspect."

"I thought Cedric was a python," Connie ventured.

"He is, ma'm. A python *is* a boa. And, as you can see, a big one. But Cedric is not your killer, Mr. Blaze. He has not left that enclosure since our arrival in Kelowna over three weeks ago."

"We only have your word on that," Blaze told him.

Meyerbaum stiffened, "If you knew your snakes, Mr. Blaze, you would know that Cedric, in or out of that enclosure, could not possibly be responsible for those deaths."

"How so?"

"The girls' bodies were recovered, were they not? Intact. If Cedric had crushed them, sir, he would also have swallowed them."

Connie blanched. "Yuck."

Blaze decided on a new approach. "I understand, Mr. Meyerbaum, that you have no special love for our Indian brothers, and that you have not been adverse to making those views known."

"They may be *your* brothers, Blaze," Meyerbaum huffed angrily, "but they sure in hell aren't mine. Sisters, neither, for that matter. Okay? The only good wahoo I ever seen," he finished vehemently, "was a dead one."

Blaze ignored the man's outburst and dug into his pocket for a business card. He scribbled an address on the back. "We have pictures of the three victims, down at Headquarters, on Doyle Street. I want you to have a look at them. Sometime today. With your specialized knowledge of snakes, you may be able to shed some light on how they died."

The snake handler bristled. "Is that an order, Blaze, or a request?"

"Take your pick," the big ex-Mountie told him evenly, "just be there."

The sun had not yet dipped behind the scorched Westside hills when the police launch came put-putting slowly along, barely raising a ripple, just off the sandy shore of Hot Sands beach. Stu Blaze stood on the bow, legs spread for balance, scanning the water ahead for the half-submerged log he had nudged out into the lake some eight hours earlier.

"Not a sign of it," he said to the officer at the wheel. "Follow through under the bridge to the south side. And keep it slow."

"Maybe it sank," Connie said helpfully from a cozy seat in the stern. She rattled the ice cubes in a tall drink and took a tentative sip.

"How'd that green-eyed gringo get on board?" Blaze growled without taking his eyes from the water.

The officer at the helm glanced back at Connie with a playful wink. "I think it's a stowaway, sir."

"Get rid of it," Blaze told him with feigned annoyance. "Tell it to take a 10-7."

Connie squealed. *10-7; out of the vehicle.* "Brute! I'm not an *it*, I'll have you know, I'm a *she*. And walking on water is not one of my best ---"

"There it is," Blaze called from the bow. He pointed ahead to where the knotty upper portion of the log was just visible above the surface of the water, glowing red in the fiery light of the rapidly sinking sun. "It must be half a mile or more from where it was this morning."

"What now?" the officer asked as he maneuvered the boat towards the log.

"We bend a line on it," Blaze told him, "and tow it back the way we came. Head for that first beach access beyond the yacht club, off Manhattan Point."

"And?"

"We turn it loose, of course."

The officer coughed softly and looked skyward. "Of course," he said.

"Stu, how'd you ever come by the name of Blaze?" Connie sat across from him, over breakfast, in a small restaurant one city block from the park. It was a brilliant, sunny Wednesday morning.

"You mean you don't know? You, of the beautiful emerald green eyes? I never told you?"

Connie felt herself blush like an adolescent. It annoyed her at times, that he could do this to her. "Nope, you never did."

"Well," Blaze said preemptively, holding a forkful of Canadian flapjack-and-sausage up for inspection before popping it into his mouth. "When my father first arrived in Canada, some fifty years ago, from the Ukraine (where else?), the name on his passport was Blazenki. Ivan Blazenki. And although he had always been proud of his name and his heritage, it didn't take him long to figure out that he'd stand a better chance in this brave new world if he dropped the *nki*, along with his accent, and his penchant for pirozshke and borsch. Losing his accent gave him the most trouble, until he met and married

17

a comely Scot immigrant who taught him to pinch his pennies and roll his *r*s. She then insisted that her first-born be called Stuart, not Ivan, and as the original Ivan Blaze humbly acquiesced, she grandly bestowed upon an unsuspecting but grateful world, the one, the only -- Stuart Blaze.'' He made a modest bow.

''How quaint,'' said an unruffled Connie, ''you've just admitted to being a mongrel.''

''Isn't everybody?''

''Yeah, but scotch and vodka? Criminy, what a mixture.''

''You're jealous,'' Blaze countered with a chuckle. ''A nasty trait. Something to do with your green eyes, I imagine.'' He gave her an irritating, but-I-forgive-you look. ''How'd you like to hear what I'm working on, with that log? I meant to fill you in last night, but it was too late.''

''Says you.'' Connie made a wry face. ''It wasn't too late for what I had in mind.'' She winked one magnificent eye at him.

''Uh-huh.'' Blaze polished off the remnants of his breakfast. ''You've got a one-tracked mind, my love.'' He pushed the dishes to one side and opened out a large map of the Okanagan Valley. ''Prepare,'' he said, ''to be edified.''

''Oh, joy.''

Blaze hunched his heavy shoulders over the table and drew a blunt finger down the length of Okanagan Lake. ''Let us first establish, that although this is, indeed, a lake, as our young constable so aptly pointed out; and while it does not possess a current, *per se*, as one would expect to find in a river; it does have an indigenous, north-to-south *flow*. Okanagan Lake, you see, is just one link in a whole chain of lakes and rivers that drain south out of the Shuswap water shed (a hundred miles to the north), down through the Okanagan Valley to the American border.''

''Mmmm.'' Connie looked thoughtful. ''If I read you right, you're about to suggest that those deaths may not have occurred off Hot Sands Beach at all.''

''Correct. But you're getting ahead of me.'' Blaze covered the map on the table with another, a more detailed blow-up of the greater

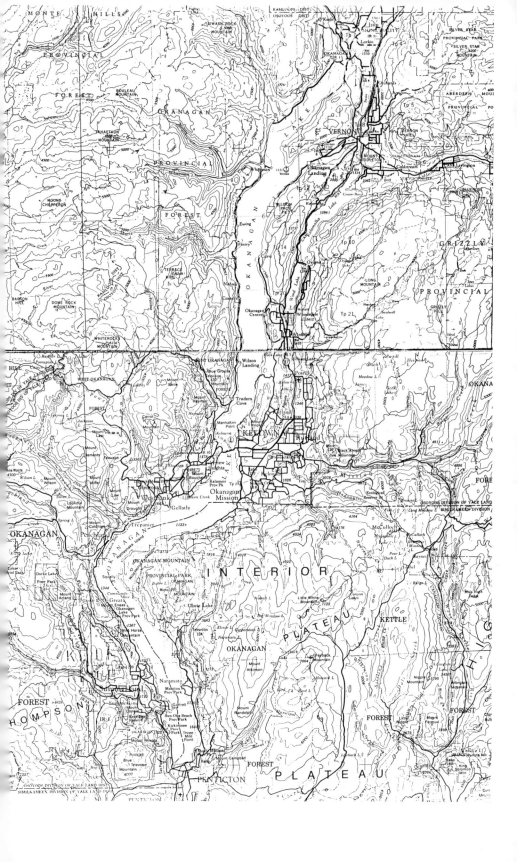

Kelowna area. "Look here, Connie, along the shoreline of the lake, going north from the bridge. First, Hot Sands beach, *here*, with the park behind it, then the yacht club, and then these two promontories of land, Manhattan Point and Poplar Point, in that order. Notice, too, that between the yacht club and Manhattan Point, it's just too cluttered to allow anyone clear access to the water's edge, and between Manhattan Point and Poplar Point, there's a string of log booms, about *here*, that would certainly impede, if not prohibit, the southerly drift of anything that might be floating in the water."

"Which," Connie followed through, "would leave Manhattan Point and Poplar Point as the only locations where a body could logically have been dumped into the lake with any reasonable expectation of having it show up at the bridge, five to eight hours later."

"You got it."

Connie tilted her pretty head expectantly. "That log we set adrift last night, off Manhattan Point. Where did it end up this morning?"

Blaze was into an all-thumbs attempt at refolding the maps. "I took a walk down there before breakfast. At about 5:30, the log had already floated past the bridge and was well on its way down the lake to where we picked it up yesterday."

So Poplar Point it is."

"Well, yes and no." He handed the maps over to Connie, still unfolded. "This whole exercise presupposes that the girls were murdered on land before being dumped into the water."

"It also presupposes that you're not giving much credence to the Ogopogo theory."

Blaze heaved a heavy sigh. "Connie, the way those girls died is so macabre, I don't think we can really presuppose anything. I guess I'm just reaching for an alternative, *any* alternative, to that of an avenging lake monster picking off Indian virgins."

"I know what you mean." Connie chewed thoughtfully at her lower lip. "Incidentally, what did Meyerbaum have to say about the pictures?"

"What else? He told Ghost that no wild creature could possibly have made those spiral bruises. They were too precise, he said, too uniform in width and spacing.

"Did he have any other solution?"

"Oh, yeah." Blaze chuckled grimly. "And just what you'd expect from Meyerbaum. He told Ghost about an old Indian method of torture, where they would tie up their victims with leather thongs that had been soaked in water, wrapped tightly around the chest and abdomen, and around the head. When the thongs dried, slowly, they shrank, and tightened ---"

"Oh, wow!"

"Oh, *Ouch!* would be more like it."

When Blaze telephoned the Tourist INFO Center at the west end of the floating bridge, he was told that Roland Rocque was a volunteer worker and only came in on Thursdays. And yes, he could probably be reached at his home, a lake-front property out on Poplar Point Drive.

"Another pig in a poke?" Connie smirked. "We do seem to be over-run with convenient irrelevancies, don't we, Mr. Blaze, sir?"

"Watch it, shorty. Nobody likes a smartass."

Nevertheless, the implications were obvious. Roland Rocque's residence proved to be the first in a row of lake-front residences beyond the point. It was conveniently situated next to an open beach-access area, where the road skirted around a sheer rock-face at lake level, then went winding up Knox Mountain's western slope to a small eagle's nest community called Herbert Heights. The house itself was sequestered behind a high laurel hedge and huddled darkly under a cover of towering conifers. A five-year old blue Ford was parked in the driveway. It was not until they were well onto the property that they noticed the fire hydrant.

"Do you see what I see?" Connie pointed a puzzled pinkie.

"You never saw a hydrant before?"

"Not in the middle of a lawn, I haven't. Especially when there's another one just like it at the end of the driveway."

Blaze shrugged it off. "This guy's supposed to be a retired fire chief, remember? Maybe the hydrant's a keepsake, or a kind of lawn ornament. Or," he grinned, "a 'happiness-is' gizmo for a pet poodle."

Connie summed it all up. "Weird," she said, "you *and* the hydrant."

Roland Rocque was not a big man, but he had a gaunt, lean look about him that would have earned him notice in any walk of life, not the least as chief of a fire department. His hair was black, and short, and straight, and his eyes lurked well back in his scull, dark and alive, like two shiny black beetles.

"Well," he said, "state your business." He spoke through his teeth, barely moving his thin lips.

Blaze hurried through the I.D. routine, with a brief explanation of why they were there. "I understand," he concluded, "that you are something of an authority on this Ogopogo thing, the lake monster."

"*N'Ha-a-itk*," Rocque admonished with apparent feeling. "And *N'Ha-a-itk* is a god, Mr. Blaze, not a monster."

"Yes, well --- if we can believe the news media, your *N'Ha-a-itk* has just taken the lives of three innocent young girls."

"Indeed he has, Mr. Blaze. And according to Indian legend, *N'Ha-a-itk* will have merely claimed his own, while they were still pure of body and heart."

Connie's eyes searched the man's strange intensity. "Do you really believe that, Mr. Rocque? Are you condoning those deaths?" She looked totally aghast. "That's nothing but an old Indian legend."

"It is not for me to question the authenticity of a legend, Miss Wells, Indian or otherwise. I am only quoting it."

"But the deaths of the three girls," Blaze persisted. "Are you seriously convinced they were the handiwork of Ogo --- uh, *N'Ha-a-itk*?"

"I would be happy to consider any alternative, Mr. Blaze. Do you have one?"

Blaze remained silent for several awkward moments. "No," he said at last, "at least, not as yet."

"Well, then. Until you do, perhaps you'd best excuse me. Sir. Madam." The swarthy ex-firechief stepped back and closed the door. Connie winced. "So much for Roll and Rock," she said.

The headlights of the van picked out the sheer rock-face beside the road as Blaze nosed the vehicle over toward the lake, onto the sandy shoulder of the beach access. Around the curve and out of sight, just a hundred yards ahead, was the cloistered house and hydrant of Roland Rocque.

As Blaze switched off the lights and motor, Connie cowered back against the seat. "Oh, horrors," she breathed in a throaty, theatrical whisper, "I know what you're up to. You've brought me to this desolate place to take advantage of me, haven't you?" She choked back a sob. "Poor me, I'm so alone and helpless --- "

Blaze reached for the door handle. "You're about as helpless as a school of caribe," he laughed.

"Keh-ree-bee? What's that?"

"Piranha, my love. Cannibal fish. They have also been known to attack men." He was out the door and headed for the lake edge.

Connie scurried in hot pursuit. "Sadist," she wailed after him. "Then why *are* we here?"

"To put this log into the lake."

Connie stopped and stared. "How'd that thing get back here?"

"I had the police launch tow it back this morning." he said, straddling the beached log. "Help me get it into the water."

Connie placed one foot either side of the log. When she stooped, her face was only inches from his. "Do piranhas kiss before they bite?" she asked as she delivered a quick peck.

Blaze gave a sudden, unassisted heave and the log slithered between her legs and into the water. Connie straightened, dusting off her hands. "What now?"

Blaze scooped her up in his massive arms and headed for the van. "Biting time," he said, baring his teeth.

Thursday morning saw Blaze, Connie, and Ghost sitting in Warfield's office, sipping coffee from styrofoam cups that Jan Thurston had brought in. When Warfield breezed through the door a few minutes later, the girl presented him with a large, steaming, china mug, with his name and rank painted on it.

"Preferential treatment," said Blaze.

"Outright discrimination," said Connie.

"Pulling rank," said Ghost.

John Warfield regarded each one in turn with feigned disaffection. "One more crack," he said, "and I'll GOA the grub."

Jan Thurston took that moment to re-enter with a plate of doughnuts. She laughed. *GOA; Gone On Arrival.* "Too late," she said, "and don't leave any for me, *please.* I'm on a diet."

"Aren't we all," Connie griped.

Warfield leaned back in his chair with his coffee in one hand, a doughnut in the other. "Well," he said, "are we any closer today, in knowing the *who,* and the *what,* and the *how,* of this Ogopogo imbroglio?"

"Imbroglio," Connie echoed softly, with an ill-advised la-di-da waggle of her pretty head.

"Yes, and no, no," Blaze said quickly in a gallant attempt to draw Warfield's attention away from his sassy cohort.

"What kind of an answer is that?" Warfield queried, with an oblique scowl at Connie.

"Yes, I do know who; and no, no, I don't know what, or how. Yet."

"You *know?*" Connie gasped. "Who --- ?"

"Roland Rocque," Ghost speculated with a murky smirk.

Blaze nodded his head. "Could be, Ghost. That guy is a 10-15 if I ever saw one." *10-15; a mental case .* "Did you run the check I called for?"

"I did." Ghost reached for his briefcase and snapped it open. He handed Blaze a brown file folder. "It's all there, Stu, and for what it's worth, Roland Rocque is not the name he was born with."

"He's an Indian, isn't he?"

"Roland Rocque?" Connie spouted in surprise. "Are you kidding?"

"Full-blooded," Ghost confirmed, with a don't-blame-me shrug at Connie. "His Indian name was Rolling Rock; hence, Roland Rocque. The first thing his mother saw at his birth must have been a highway sign. Happily, she left off the 'Watch For.' The name change, by the way, was done legally."

Blaze rifled the file impatiently. "Give us a verbal on this, will you, Ghost?"

"Okay. Here it is in a nutshell. Rocque grew up on a reservation. He was educated in one of those typical Indian schools they had scattered around the interior. When he was of age, he joined the Canadian Army, went overseas in '39, and stayed on when the war ended. He kept his nose clean and struggled up through the ranks to non-com, a sergeant, in charge of Fire Detail. He never married. When his hitch was up, he took his pension, and, on the strength of his army training, applied for a job --- Fire Chief, in Osoyoos. That's a small Okanagan border town, just over the line from Oroville, Washington, about seventy-five miles south of here."

"I though that was a volunteer unit," Warfield interjected, "in Osoyoos, I mean."

"It is. Or, at least, it was. At the time, the chief was the only one who drew a salary. Anyway, after a couple of smoke-filled years, Rocque was finally caught setting his own fires and summarily canned."

"Figures," Blaze grunted.

Warfield rang for more coffee. "What makes you think he's our man, Stu?"

"Well --- " Blaze paused for a refill from Jan Thurston. "For a case to be this weird, John, there has to be a weirdo in it somewhere. And for my money, you'll go a long way before you find anyone weirder than Rocque. Something must have toppled his teepee when he was down in Osoyoos and began lighting those fires, and unless I miss my guess, he's been on his own private little warpath ever since. I'm just surprised they didn't plunk him in the pokey then."

"They knew he was guilty," Ghost said, "but they couldn't prove it in court."

"Yeah." Blaze heaved a sigh. "Join the club."

"But what have you actually got, Stu," Warfield persisted, "that ties Rocque to these killings?"

"Nothing definite, John. Call it a hunch if you like, but it's really more than that. Everything just seems to keep pointing in his direction. Take the victims, for a start. They were female, young, and naked; but they weren't sexually molested. Doesn't figure. Maybe they were sacrificial lambs, eh? A big step up, I'll admit, from chickens and pigs, but not unfeasible. And, even more to the point, they were all Indians. Rocque is an Indian. Ogopogo (aka *N'Ha-a-itk*) is an Indian legend. In fact, from where I sit, this whole snafu has an Indian calling card on it."

Blaze paused to sip his coffee.

"Keep talking," Warfield told him.

"Yeah, well --- there seems to be a uniformity and precision to every mother-lovin' facet of this case. Ritualistic, almost; or, you could say, militaristic. Rocque, again, on both counts. Think about it: all three bodies were found on consecutive Friday mornings, all in the same general area; they all died in the same bizarre way, and were in the water for the same relative length of time. Even the spiral bruises, as Meyerbaum pointed out, on all three girls, were curiously equidistant from neck to knee."

"I guess that rules out Ogopogo as the culprit," Ghost put in, "or, for that matter, any other wild creature. All that leaves us now, is Meyerbaum's 'wet-thong' theory."

"As flaky as it sounds, Ghost, it's the only solution, thus far, that runs consistent with the autopsy reports. And it *is* something that Rocque would know about. I think you'd better have a look inside that house, out at Poplar Point, but wait until he leaves for the Tourist INFO Center. This is his day to be there and I don't want to tip our hand."

Ghost drifted to his feet. "In the meantime, where will you be?"

"Connie and I will be tied to Rocque like a tin can to a cat's tail." Blaze turned to his green-eyed confederate. "I checked out that log this morning," he told her. "It was at the bridge, right about where the girls' bodies were found. There's no doubt now, in my mind, that those kids were dumped, dead, into the lake, somewhere out at Poplar Point."

"Then what do you hope to prove by tailing Rocque?" the inspector queried. "Why not just stake out the Point?"

"It's too late for that, John." Blaze levered himself out of his chair. "Whatever happened to those girls had to begin during the day prior to the discovery of their bodies. And there just has to be some connection between the killings and Rocque's volunteer stint at the INFO Center. If Rocque *is* our man, and he strikes again on schedule, he should be lining up his fourth victim sometime in the next twelve hours. I'd like to be there when he does."

"And if Rocque is not our man?"

"Then tomorrow morning," Blaze said grimly, "instead of a log, we'd better look for another dead Indian."

The better part of three hours had elapsed since they had pulled in and parked within easy viewing distance of Rocque's blue Ford. Connie sat sweating it out beside Blaze in a gray, unmarked Plymouth (the air-conditioned van would have been too conspicuous), watching an endless flow of tourists come and go from the INFO Center at the west end of Okanagan Lake bridge. They were dressed for the part --- Connie in olive-green shorts and a tank top, Blaze in white slacks and T-shirt --- looking like any other vacationing couple in the ever-changing conflux of cars and people.

"The Ogopogo hype might be keeping people out of the lake," Connie said, stifling a yawn, "But it hasn't done much to dampen the flow of traffic over the bridge."

"There are plenty of other lakes and recreational attractions in the valley," Blaze reminded her. "But, not to worry, my love, Ogopogo won't be wearing the villain's hat much longer."

"You truly are convinced that Rocque is behind those horrible killings, aren't you?"

"I am."

"Then how did he do it, Stu? And *why*?"

"I don't know yet. And even when I do, I don't expect the why of it to make any sense to anyone but Rocque, himself. And *N'Ha-a-itk*, maybe. As for the how? Well, let's wait and see what Ghost comes up with."

"Not much," said a gray voice behind them. The faint click of a door handle and the almost imperceptible dip of the car's springs had preceded the words by a split second.

Connie spun on her olive-green axis. "My God, Ghost. You do have a way of --- popping up."

Blaze chuckled. "How'd you find us, Ghost?"

"You're sitting in my car, remember?"

"This isn't a car, it's a sauna on wheels." Blaze wiped the perspiration from his forehead with the back of a thick wrist. "What'd you find out at Poplar Point?"

"The house is an Indian museum, Stu. The walls are covered with portraits of legendary Indian chiefs; Sitting Bull, Crazy Horse, Cochise, Running Bear. Scenes of historic Indian battles, including a dozen or more of the ever infamous Little Bighorn. Old Indian beads and bric-a-brac, souvenirs, arrowheads, snowshoes, peacepipes. You name it. Everything but a squaw in a wigwam."

"Nothing besides memorabilia?"

"Food (dried herbs, pemmican, stuff like that), a few books, clothing. That's about it."

"In the attic, or basement?"

"No attic, just a crawl. Nothing. Half-basement on a split-level. Nothing." Ghost scratched at his gray grizzle of hair. "There *was* one thing, Stu. An old fire hose. In the basement. And, uh -- a couple of odd-looking, castiron ring-bolts, about four inches in diameter and spaced six or seven feet apart, embedded in the concrete floor."

"Hmm. Sounds like the house was built on a mooring slab. Nothing else? Nothing unusual?"

"A fire hose isn't unusual?"

"Not to an ex-fire-chief. What about the hydrant?"

"It's the real thing, Stu. They changed the property line when Rocque bought the place. Something to do with updating an old survey. Anyway, they installed a new hydrant out on the road allowance, and just didn't bother to take the old one out.''

"Is it hooked up?"

"Yep. According to City Works. But like the guy said, "who cares?"

"Anything else?"

"Yeah." Ghost dug into his pocket and handed over a small polybag that contained what looked to be a short coil of blackened metal.

"What is it?"

"A zipper, I think. It's pretty well burned. I found it out back, in one of those forty-five gallon drums, the kind they use for burning rubbish. Might just be one of Rocque's.''

"Uh-huh." Blaze held the bag up to the light. "And then again, it might not.''

It was late in the afternoon when Connie first noticed the young Indian girl, walking slowly down the long west hill toward the bridge. She wore blue jeans and a faded yellow blouse. And even from a distance, Connie could identify the high delicate cheek bones, the Oriental eyes, the long, lank blue-black hair. A limp canvas tote-bag was slung over one shoulder. She could not have been more than fifteen years old.

When the girl drew abreast of the INFO Center's parking area, she paused shyly to contemplate a bevy of kids her own age, Caucasian, well-dressed and well-fed, and there was a look of stoic envy in her dark eyes. When they noticed her watching, the girl turned away, walking slowly on toward the bridge and Kelowna.

Connie sighed, intoning and paraphrasing the old chestnut: *"Poor little lamb who has lost her way."*

"It isn't so much that they stray from the flock," Blaze said, waxing philosophical, "it's that the flock just doesn't have enough shepherds.''

"Did *we*, when we were that age?"

"Oh, I think so. At least we were given a hell of a lot better chance of survival than they get. We're still living in a world of racial bigotry, Connie, and like it or not, no one of us is blameless or totally immune."

"Oooo. You sound grim."

"Not so grim as I feel. I just can't forget that three innocent kids have died, and we're faced with the chronological threat of there being a fourth, tonight. I feel as though I'm between the devil and a dead place."

"Speak of the devil," Connie said, pointing. "There's our renegade redskin."

Roland Rocque had emerged from the INFO Center and was headed briskly toward his car. In seconds, he was behind the wheel of the blue Ford, intimidating his way out into the flow of bridge traffic. A dozen cars slipped by before Blaze could get the gray Plymouth into line behind him.

"He's sure in an all-fired hurry," Connie noted, craning her head to hold him in view. "Wait," she said suddenly, "he's pulling over, stopping, right on the bridge," then a plaintive, "oh, *no.*"

The traffic wormed its way around the flashing rear lights of the stalled Ford, and just as the Plymouth drew abreast, Blaze caught a glimpse of the Indian girl's dark head disappearing into the open, passenger-side door.

"Sacrificial lamb number four," Blaze muttered under his breath.

As they left the bridge, Blaze hung a hard right at the first intersection, then did a quick, illegal U-y. He parked facing the traffic, at right angles to the bridge. The Ford went by as the light changed and Blaze swung in behind it, holding back to let a station wagon full of kids and camping gear move between them.

"My god," Connie breathed, hunching forward against the dash, "whatever you do, don't lose them."

The Ford turned left at the third traffic light, heading north. Blaze followed. "Right on cue." he said grimly. "Poplar Point, here we come."

It was as though the sun had fallen with a great splash into a pool of blood, drenching the western sky with diverging streaks of crimson. As far as one could see, from the placid surface of the lake to the crests of the low-lying mountains, from the city's indigenous sprawl to the surrounding hillside quilts of farms and orchards, everything had taken on the sanguinary hue of the dying day.

"It looks positively ominous," Connie said in a small hushed voice. "I'm not normally superstitious, but ---"

"But, *what*? For Pete's sake, Connie. First Warfield with his stupid smoke signals, now you." Blaze snorted with exasperation. "All I need now is for Ghost to come up with a hot tip from a Ouija board."

"I heard that, you hunky heretic."

The van was parked at the lake edge, out of sight of the Rocque property. Blaze sat in the front seat monitoring the two-way AM/FM radio receiver, built into the dash and crystal-tuned to pick up Ghost's small portable hand unit. Connie huddled beside him, chewing her nails. The gray voice had emanated from the speaker.

"I read you, Ghost. What's up?"

A crackle of static, then, "Nothing yet, Stu. I'm within fifteen feet of the fire hydrant, like you wanted, and I'm out of sight. But tell me ---"

"Well?"

"What am I *doing* here?"

"Sooner or later, Ghost, Rocque is going to show up out there, and I want you to nab him."

"Sure, but why? Why don't we just go in and get him?"

"I'll explain later. Just don't let him get too close to that fire hydrant."

There was the sound of a long painful sigh. "Over and out, Blazenki."

Connie handed Blaze a cup of coffee from a steaming thermos. "You know how he killed those girls, don't you?" she said quietly.

"Yes."

"I don't suppose you'd like to --- "

"Later."

Connie poured herself a coffee, then focused her green eyes on him through the rising steam. "Is she safe, in there?"

"For the moment."

"But why, Stu? Why put her through it? Why don't we move in like Ghost says?"

"We don't have enough on him, that's why. Not yet. When we take this guy in, Connie, I want him to stay in. For keeps."

"But, Stu, that poor girl ---"

"She'll get over it." Blaze opened the glove compartment and drew out an old service revolver from his army days, a Smith & Wesson .38, mounted on a Colt frame. He spun the loaded cylinder and set the gun up on the dash, within easy reach. "It'll give the kid something to tell her grandchildren," he added without humor.

The Okanagan twilight was a slow but total process. Red to rusty gray, gray to velvet black. And the heat of the day seemed to drain off over the lip of the horizon with the last vestiges of light. Connie shivered in her olive-green shorts.

"I think I'll change into something warmer while I've got the chance," she told Blaze. Then, later, in jeans and sweater, she stewed through another hour of edge-of-the-seat horripilation before Ghost finally sounded the alarm.

"Movement at the west side basement window-well, Stu." Ghost's muted voice sounded like he was calling a golf game at Rancho Mirage. "He's shoving something out. Damn, I can't make out what it is."

"Stay with it, Ghost." Blaze reached for the .38, checked the safety, and shoved it under his belt. No domelight came on as he opened the door and left it ajar.

Seconds dragged into minutes, then, *crackle*, "He's coming out the side door, Stu. Now he's going over to the window. What the---? He's hauling one end of that damn hose out to the hydrant. And, Stu --- *Jeeeez!* You should *see* the guy."

"Tell me."

"All he's got on is a loin cloth and moccasins. And he's got war paint smeared all over --- "

Blaze was out the door and running, Connie close behind with surprising drive and speed. They broke through the encircling hedge almost in unison, then braked to a startled stop before a moon-lit scene that had all the makings of a B-run Western.

Ghost was face down on the lawn, his head bloodied. The near-naked Rocque poised above him, all paint and feathers, a tomahawk raised above his head. Blaze fired from the hip and the Indian gave a whoop of pain. The tomahawk made a slow, harmless arc over Ghost's head and buried itself in the lawn. Rocque dropped to one knee, hugging his right wrist.

Connie, following the path of the bullet, pounced on the wounded redskin with cuffs at the ready. But Rocque wasn't done yet. As one handcuff clicked onto his damaged wrist, he shot his arm up, over Connie's head, forcing the linking chain of the cuffs tight against her throat. He held it there with his good arm and turned to face Blaze.

"An Indian stand-off," Blaze muttered. He glared threateningly, but Rocque was implacable. He tightened the chain and waited. One sharp tug, Blaze knew, could break Connie's neck.

Ghost was beginning to stir on the lawn and Blaze used the distraction to edge closer. But Rocque caught the movement and swung obliquely to them, keeping both men in view. "Back off," he snarled.

It was then that Connie became a sudden, unexpected blur of movement. She drove her queenly butt back into Rocque's midsection, knocking him off balance. Then with her hands cupping his, to take the pressure off her neck, she powered her whole hundred and seventeen pounds down towards Mother Earth. Rocque's gaunt frame took to the air, twisting above her in a tight, punishing jack-knife. Before the Indian touched terra-firma, Blaze was on him.

The highway was heavy with traffic as the black van headed out of Kelowna, north on 97. Blaze was at the wheel, his rugged, boyish

face wreathed in his usual, post-case, 'Well,-I'm-glad-that's-over'
look.

Connie arched an auburn eyebrow at him, "I'd never have
guessed." She wore jeans and a shirt of white denim. A white cloth
choker circled her bruised throat.

"How's the neck?" Blaze asked.

"It *has* seen better days." Her voice was an unintended sexy
whisper. "You'll just have to be a little inventive when you make
passionate love to me."

"I'll keep that in mind."

They rode in silence for some time, until Connie pointed out the
window to a long, narrow stretch of water that was slipping by on their
right. "That must be Kalamalka Lake. Jan Thurston told me to watch
for it." The lake's mirror-like surface was a kaleidoscope of colors;
blues and greens, and swirling florescent ribbons of turquoise.

"The lake was named after an Indian chief," Connie expounded
huskily, "Kalamalka, which actually translates to mean the colorful
velvet stage in the growth of a deer's antlers, but, time and tribe seem
to have deferred to a somewhat more liberal interpretation, 'Lake of
Many Colors,' a *nom-de guerre* by which it is now widely known."

"Your French-Canadian slip is showing," Blaze told her sardoni-
cally.

"I'm only half French."

"Oh?"

"On my mother's side."

"And the other?"

"Welsh."

"So you're a half-breed, just like me."

"Two of a kind," Connie rasped. "When we get married, we'll
have quarter-breed kids and octonocular grandchildren who'll be able
to look eight ways before crossing the street."

Blaze rolled his eyes toward Mountie heaven. "Anyway," he
conceded, "I am impressed with this place. It certainly lives up to its
licence-plate logo: *Beautiful British Columbia*. I hate to be leaving
so soon."

"We'll be back soon enough for the trial," Connie reminded him. She put a tentative hand to her bruised throat. "By the way, how is Ghost this morning?"

"Not what you'd call in the pink," Blaze chuckled, "but with Ghost, wan is wonderful. Rocque's tomahawk left him with a mild concussion and a scalp-raising headache, but he'll be okay."

"Thank God." Connie shuddered. "I can still see that poor girl, Stu, in the basement, all wound up in the fire hose. She was scared stiff."

"Wouldn't you be?"

"I guess. Not to mention, embarrassed. But I don't understand how he actually did that. You know, with the hose."

"Have you ever tried to hang onto the working end of one of those fire hoses?"

"No, of course not."

"It sometimes takes two, even three strong men, Connie, just to keep the nozzle pointed in the right direction. Water is incompressible, that's a natural law; its hydraulic force can be devastating. What Rocque did, in effect, was to harness that power in about twenty feet of hose, to make it look as though *N'Ha-a-itk* had, indeed, claimed his virgin brides."

"That I know, but ---"

"After positioning his victim between the two ring bolts in the basement, Connie, then wrapping her tightly with the flattened fire hose, he simply capped and anchored one end to one bolt, then passed the other end through the other bolt and out to the hydrant. When he turned on the valve, swelling the hose with water, an unrelenting, bone-crushing pressure of almost a hundred pounds to the square inch was exerted along the entire length of the hose. It truly must have been like being crushed by a giant snake; or, as Rocque fantasized, by *N'Ha-a-itk*. Not a pleasant way to die."

"Is dying ever pleasant?" Connie wondered with an appropriate shiver. "What mystifies me, though, is how he got those young girls out of their clothes and into the basement. We know they were conscious when they died, and no kid, however, naive, would ever submit willingly to anything so---so grotesque.''

''We may never know, Connie, but my guess is they were drugged. And yes, I'm well aware the autopsy tests drew a blank, but unless the lab knows what to look for, a rare or obscure drug can often go undetected. They're still analyzing those dried herbs Ghost found in Rocque's house, as well as blood samples taken from the girl we rescued last night. If there's drug residue in either one, they'll find it.''

Connie turned with a frown. ''Aren't we leaving a little prematurely, Stu? I mean, it's like turning our backs on a hanging before they spring the trap. They still haven't finished sifting the ashes where Rocque burned the girls' clothing.''

''Not to worry, Connie. We caught him red-handed (if you'll pardon the pun) and this drug thing, plus whatever turns up in the ashes, is all icing on the cake. The only problem now, will be to insulate Rocque from the do-gooders and the shrinks. If that bunch get their way, they'll slap him on the wrist, tell him 'naughty, naughty', and turn him loose in six months.''

''*N'importe.* We've done our part.'' Connie yawned prettily; she'd heard it all before. ''Where are we going now?''

''Home, where else?''

''Calgary? That's quite a trip, Stu. It's a long time to be cooped up in this van --- alone --- just you and me --- together. Don't you think we ought to get married first?''

''And spoil a beautiful friendship?''

Connie snorted in exasperation. ''You might just as well capitulate now, Stuart Blaze. It's only a question of time, you know.''

''Think so?''

She levelled her beautiful green eyes at him. ''Even *ex*-Mounties get their man, *mon cher.*''

OGOPOGO
Fact or Fantasy

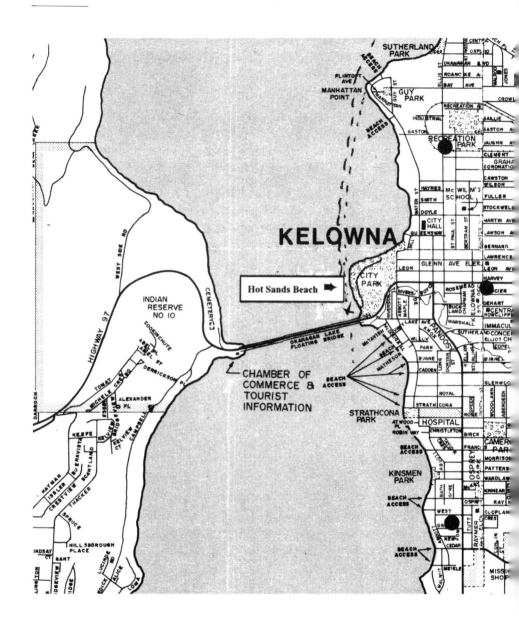

OKANAGAN LAKE

OGOPOGO
Fact or Fantasy

Long before the white man came to the Okanagan Valley, in the heart of what we know now as *Beautiful British Columbia*, the legendary lake monster was alive and well. He, she, *it* --- was known to the aboriginal inhabitants of the time as *N'Ha-a-itk*, or, loosely translated, *Devil Of The Lake*. It was believed to reside in a watery cave off Squally Point, a turbulent stretch of water across from what is now the modern town of Peachland. The burning question is: is *N'Ha-a-itk* still in residence?

Crypto-zoologists, who have investigated the region, believe the underwater serpent to be a descendant of a marine dinosaur, left over from the Ice Age, and related to the species *Basilosaurus Cetoipts*, a benevolent creature of old that fed primarily (but not exclusively) on lake vegetation. Scientists also believe that the lake monster is one of as many as thirty-six other aquatic phenomena that currently inhabit the planet, mainly in the environs of the fiftieth parallel, and, in those bodies of water that are excessively deep. Interestingly enough, the fiftieth parallel intersects Lake Okanagan a mile or two north of the City of Kelowna, and the depth of the water at that point has been sounded at over one thousand feet.

Food for thought.

Legend has it that the early natives rarely ventured out on *N'Ha-a-itk*-infested waters without a chicken or a small pig, or even a dog, stashed in the bottom of their birch bark canoes. These sacrificial 'lambs' were used to toss over the side at an opportune time, to appease or otherwise distract their resident omnivore long enough to ensure safe passage. It must be remembered that these early people did not have the expertise of university-trained crypto-zoologists on whom to rely for guidance in adopting a 'safety-first' policy while rubbing elbows, so to speak, with *N'Ha-a-itk*. Nevertheless, it could well be said that aboriginal smarts did successfully rule the day; while *N'Ha-a-itk*, in its own natatorial way, continued to rule the waves.

With the coming of the white man, it was soon deemed prudent not to entrust the history of these visual encounters with the lake monster to tribal elders spinning tales around a campfire. Just how many sightings it took to get the historical record started, is not known, but even in those unenlightened days, the fear of ridicule must have given pause to many who thought they had seen the serpent, but never had the temerity to make their secret known. That dubious honor, of being the first Caucasian to record visual contact with *N'Ha-a-itk*, eventually fell to a Mrs. Susan Allison, in 1872. Those who later bravely followed her example now number in the hundreds.

What did *N'Ha-a-itk* look like? Well, it was a ''fearsome thing,'' according to those who had seen it, ''dark green in color,'' we are told, ''a snake-like body, about fifteen to twenty feet long,'' and with ''a bearded, horse-like or goat-like head.'' Not something one would want to come upon unexpectedly in the dark deep waters of the lake, especially in the lingering, swirling, obfuscating mists of an Okanagan twilight.

It was not until 1942 that the legendary *N'Ha-a-itk* adopted the name of OGOPOGO, an appellation that, unlike its Indian eponym, was imposed frivolously upon the monster and bore no scientific or historical significance. But the name stuck! It was almost as though the monster itself had spoken:

''*Ogopogo is now my name*
And monstering will be my game.''

Well, be that as it may; the fact remains that Ogopogo has since become as famous, or nearly so, as its Scottish cousin, *Nessie*, the notorious Loch Ness Monster. The renowned insurance firm, Lloyd's Of London, eventually added to Ogopogo's international recognition by underwriting a policy on the reclusive reptile for the principal sum of one million dollars; the entire face value of the policy to go to anyone who could furnish living proof of the creature's existence. And shortly thereafter; the Monster, the Myth, and the Million Dollar Bounty, was written into *Hansard* in the House of Commons in Ottawa, at the behest of the local Member Of Parliament from Okanagan Boundary.

Talk about a *Plesiosaurus* with *Pizzazz*!

The on-going, ever-burgeoning mystique of Ogopogo is perpetuated on an annual basis by the Okanagan Similkameen Tourist Association and the Okanagan Valley's collective Chambers of Commerce. The ensuing hype is augmented further still by visiting biologists, zoologists, and oceanographers, together with countless hordes of tourists and curiosity seekers. A television crew from Japan recently filmed a documentary featuring Ogopogo (in 1990). The resulting film was televised in Japan and met with such success that the crew was back again in 1991 for another shot at it. This time, they brought along sonic-detection gear, underwater cameras, a miniature one-man submarine, a helicopter, and a preponderance of other related paraphernalia. They are scheduled to air this second, more comprehensive film on Japanese television to an estimated eighty million viewers, on a program called *The World's Supernatural Phenomena*. American television, too, has jumped into the act, utilizing assorted segments of video footage, photographs and eyewitness accounts of sightings that were subsequently shown on two popular television series, *Unsolved Mysteries* and *Inside Edition*.

Still, at the height of all this notoriety, it must be said, in all fairness, that Ogopogo is not what you can rightly call a *fait accompli*. Sceptics abound, in both the native and the non-native communities. There are those who scoff at the very idea of a 'monster' lurking in the placid depths of the valley's largest and most beautiful lake. But the faithful are quick to point to the hundreds of meticulously documented sightings, by credible, rational people. How can that many people be wrong? In the final analysis, one must conclude, it all boils down to the old adage, *Seeing is believing.*

The Author

Photos Courtesy of:
Kelowna Daily Courier

While Japanese film crews were searching diligently for Ogopogo with their phalange of high-tech paraphernalia, on March 7, 1991, local workmen near Kelowna facetiously leaked a rumor that they would be taking Ogopogo "for a walk" the next morning. The accompanying photo was the hilarious denouement. The in-take pipe was actually destined for the West Bank Indian reserve. The Ogopogo head? Courtesy of Don Claughton.

MEL D. AMES

"SEEING IS BELIEVING"

A CHRONOLOGY OF OGOPOGO SIGHTINGS AS DOCUMENTED BY *THE KELOWNA CHAMBER OF COMMERCE* AND MADE AVAILABLE THROUGH THE COURTESY OF *THE OKANAGAN SIMILKAMEEN TOURIST ASSOCIATION*

	DATE	SIGHTED BY:	LOCATION
(1)	1872	Mrs. Susan Allison	Westbank
(2)	1890	Captain Thomas Short	Squally Point
(3)	1900	H.B.D. Lysons	Rattlesnake Island
(4)	1923	Captain Matt Reid	Rattlesnake Island
(5)	1931	Mrs. Mary Gartrell	Trout Creek Point
(6)	1936	Geoffrey Tozer	Mission Creek
(7)	1940	Mr. Smith	Naramata
(8)	1946	Mrs. Kay Bissett	Summerland
(9)	1950	A.W. Gray	Squally Point
(10)	1951	Monty De Mara	Squally Point
(11)	1958	William Marks	Casa Loma Point
(12)	1962	Jack Lowe	Poplar Point
(13)	1973	Mrs. Hurd	City Park
(14)	1974	Mrs. Gwen Evans	Penticton
(15)	1977	Jillian Fletcher	Scottish Cove
(16)	1977	Sandy Ripple	Coral Beach
(17)	1978	Emil Puffalt	Okanagan Landing
(18)	1978	Ethel London	Kinsmen Beach
(19)	1979	Arlene Gaal	Rattlesnake Island
(20)	1983	Frank Penner	Mission Creek

44

DATE	SIGHTED BY:		LOCATION
(21)	1984	Yvonne Svennsson	Paul's Tomb
(22)	1984	Bill Trakalo	Peachland
(23)	1984	David Methedal	Peachland
(24)	7/1987	Michel Tabori	North of Floating
(25)	7/1987	Victor Nelli Jr.	ABC film crew (Secrets &
		-David Frank	Mysteries Show) video
		-Gerry Fredrick	taped actual sighting.
(25)	5/1987	Phylis Frew	Mission Hill Winery
		John Kirk & Family	Video taped: 8:15-8:40 pm
(26)	7/1988	W. & S. Alsup	Near Fintry (3 photos)
(27)	9/1988	Nahirney Family	Boating 10 m. from bridge
(28)	7/1989	John Kirk &	Peach Orchard Beach
		John Kirk, Jr.	Summerland Peach Orchard. In view: one minute
(29)	1989	Ken Chapman	Bear Creek Provincial Park

The last sighting documented above was shared with millions of television viewers across North America, both north and south of the border. Ken Chapman and his son committed their famous sighting to posterity with a video tape which was subsequently seen as part of the TV series, *Unsolved Mysteries*.

There have been many sightings since Ken Chapman's in 1989, and there will be many more recorded in the future. To add your own name to this growing list, reserve a seat on the scenic shores of Lake Okanagan, by writing or telephoning for information regarding tourist facilities and accommodations in Beautiful British Columbia's Okanagan Valley:

THE OKANAGAN SIMILKAMEEN TOURIST ASSOCIATION
#104-515 Highway 97 South
KELOWNA, B.C., Canada V1Z 3J2
Tel: (604) 769-5959 Fax: (604) 861-7493

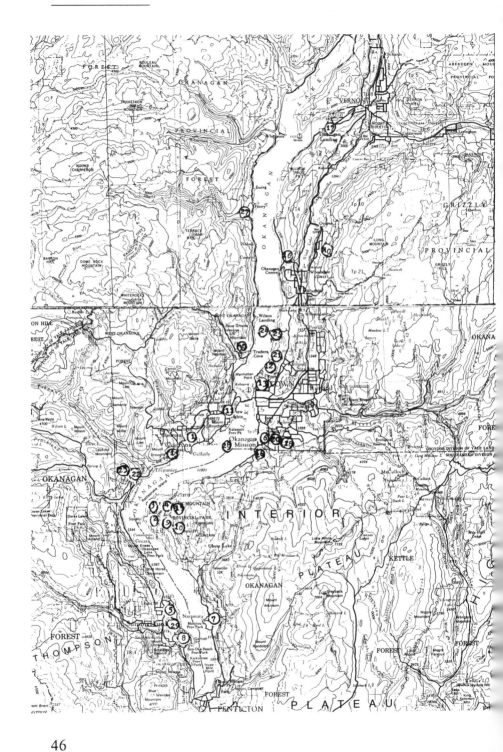

OKANAGAN LAKE FROM SOUTH

Photo courtesy of: Kelowna Museum Archives

A peaceful, unspoiled view of Lake Okanagan in the early years
following the turn of the century. *N'Ha-a-itk* was reportedly then still
enjoying notoriety among the native people, and continued to do so
until *Ogopopo* took over in 1942. Now, half a century later, the
monster (by whatever name) still haunts the depths of the lake with
impunity.

Photo courtesy of: Kelowna Museum Archives

A view of one of the rocky outcroppings along Lake Okanagan's multifaceted shoreline. The photograph is thought to have been taken near Grant's Tomb, looking north, and is eerily similar to the legendary site of Ogopogo's watery lair near Squally Point.

Photo courtesy of: Kelowna Museum Archives

A typical photograph of Lake Okanagan and indicative of the many
that have surfaced in recent years, showing "unexplained ridges or
humps" in the otherwise placid water. A sure sign of Ogopogo's
dragon-like presence. Literally hundreds of these 'sightings' have
been recorded since 1872.

49

MEL D. AMES

THE COLORFUL PAST OF
OGOPOGO RECALLED

On August 16, 1989, staff writer, Neil Godbout, of the KELOWNA
CAPITAL NEWS wrote:
Picture this: A man stands up at a Rotary Club Luncheon
in Vernon in 1926 and sings this song:
"I'm looking for the Ogopogo,
the bunny-hugging Ogopogo.
His mother was a mutton,
his father was a whale.
I'm going to put a little bit
of salt on his tail.
I'm looking for the Ogopogo."

W.H. Brimblecombe sang that tune which he took from a popular
English melody. Brimblecombe's version was nearly identical except
that the British wanted to find Ogopogo while he was "playing his old
banjo."
Brimblecombe thought Ogopogo would be a delightfully silly
name for the lake monster everyone was talking about. So did the
Vancouver Province, who in the following day's paper, declared
Ogopogo to be the "official" name of Okanagan Lake's aquatic
monster.
Ogopogo sightings that same summer were a local sensation with
new sightings reported almost every week. One story has a visiting
chief named *Timbasket* canoeing out onto the lake with his family

without a sacrifice to prove his bravery and to show there was no monster. The canoe suddenly disappeared in the middle of the lake.

The stories continued with the arrival of settlers into the valley, and others were resurrected from the past. In 1854, a Metis man was crossing the lake in his canoe with some horses in tow when suddenly one of the horses was tugged under the water. The man had to cut the rope free from his canoe or be dragged down himself.

When the B.C. government announced a ferry boat to run between Kelowna and Westbank in the summer of 1926, it said the ship would be "armed with devices designed to repel attacks from Mr. Ogopogo."

Around the same time, some big game hunters from around the province and Washington were congregating around the lake, hoping to shoot the terrible beast. They gave up quickly.

However, some shots *were* taken at Ogopogo by a man on Carr's Landing in July 1949. A startled editor at the Kelowna newspaper asked Attorney-General Gordon Wismer to put Ogopogo on the list of animals not to be shot at. Wismer assured Kelowna residents that Ogopogo was protected under Section 26 of the Fisheries Act.

The Canadian Tourist Association offered $5,000 for genuine photographic evidence. A $1,000,000 prize was offered in 1984 by the Okanagan-Similkameen Tourist Association to capture Ogopogo alive with a rod and reel.

Excerpted from an article
by staff writer Neil Godbout
of the Kelowna Capital News

Photo courtesy: Kelowna Capital I

Tourists and local children exhibit little fear of a sculptured likeness of OGOPOGO lounging near the Fintry Queen at the entrance to City Park.

KELOWNA CITY COUNCIL
PONDERS OGOPOGO'S PLURALITY

Kelowna City Council took an unprecedented detour in city politics in the summer of 1989 when council members were persuaded to solicit the help of the provincial and federal governments in protecting their local lake monster.

Ogopogo, it was determined, was an endangered species and needed protection from unspecified 'senseless acts' of aggression from certain segments of society.

Mayor Jim Stuart stated that he would not 'feel silly' in seeking the required financial and moral support of those two august bodies.

All council members then watched a film of what appeared (to the majority of their electorate) to be nothing more, nor less, than a beaver flopping about and flapping its tail in some cloistered corner of the lake, but the most controversial debate was centered on how to pluralize the creature's name, should more than one eventually surface at the same time --- Ogopogos? Ogopogoes? Ogopogi?

The one most embarrassed by all this 'silliness' is probably Ogopogo, himself, uh --- herself? --- itself?

Or maybe even, themselves?

Silly, isn't it?

filming a segment on our
mythical lake creature.

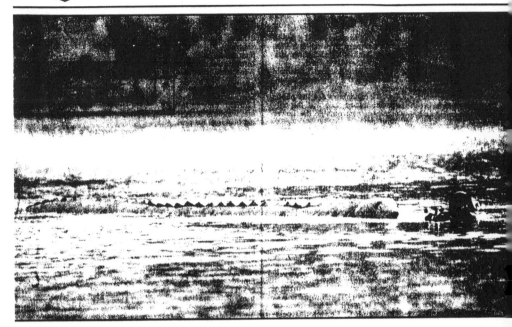

Ogopogo, the television mode

Courtesy of:
Kelowna Daily Cour

"It swims in a straight line.
It wriggles back and forth.
It bobs in the water.
It looks like --- Ogopogo!"

An excerpt from same-day
article by J.P. Squire -
Courier Staff

WILL THE REAL OGOPOGO PLEASE
STAND UP ---

When the popular television series UNSOLVED MYSTERIES decided to do a number on Ogopogo, they weren't taking any chances. They constructed their own version of the infamous lake monster just in case the 'original' turned out to be camera shy.

The bogus Ogopogo was eighteen feet long, with saw-tooth fins along its back and a head that looked more like a polar bear's than that of an aquatic serpent.

It moved in worm-like fashion, however, with the choreographed help of three scuba divers working in harmony beneath the surface. Then, to further enhance the illusion of authenticity, a number of scenes were recreated from accounts of past sightings, from as far back as 1854 and as recent as tomorrow.

Little wonder that with the expertise of present-day filmmakers in the art of 'special effects' (aka visual deception), it did not present much of a challenge for UNSOLVED MYSTERIES to dupe a gullible generation of couch potatoes into believing they were seeing the real thing.

Nevertheless, in spite of the obvious sham, the original OGOPOGO will undoubtedly continue to haunt the murky depths of Lake Okanagan, undeterred.

THE NAHIRNEY SIGHTING

This 'sighting' of Ogopogo has been singled out for special mention by the author because of its unique clarity and the high credibility of those who witnessed the event:

Denise Nahirney, museum co-ordinator
Bill Nahirney, mechanical engineer
Lynnette Nahirney, tour guide (daughter)
Mary Kolibab, Bill Nahirney's sister
Lawrence Kolibab, Mary's husband

It was the afternoon of September 3rd, 1988, a beautiful sunny Okanagan day, when the Nahirneys and the Kolibabs took to the calm waters of Lake Okanagan in Lawrence Kolibab's 18 foot speed boat for a family outing. They had cruised north, uneventfully, to a point about 10 miles from Kelowna's floating bridge, before changing course toward the distant western shoreline. And it was *there*, where the depths of the lake had previously been sounded at close to 165 fathoms (about 1000 feet) that they were joined by a seemingly indifferent escort, swimming parallel to the boat about 200 feet off their bow.

"Just prior to this encounter," Denise Nahirney recalls, "there seemed to be any number of other boats about, but once we spotted the 'creature', we suddenly realized we were all alone with whatever it was in the water." They were moving at a "good clip" and it was Bill, keeping a sharp lookout for perilous dead-heads (submerged logs) who first spotted their uninvited guest, but seconds later, all eyes in the boat were glued to the awesome sight.

Mary Kolibab readily admits to being "scared stiff" and Lynnette Nahirney does not deny putting caution ahead of valor by moving back in the boat, closer to her father. It was Denise Nahirney, with the inherent curiosity of a curator, who has since put living flesh and bone to the thing in the water, in minute and colorful detail.

"It was keeping pace with us," she says, "three large humps with an indistinct half-hidden head, moving through the water like a partially submerged submarine. It must have been 40 feet long," she estimates, "with a thick, round, dinosaur-type body. It caused the boat to rock and pitch over the wash of its rapidly rising wake."

Denise's voice, as she recounted the experience, was laden with a sense of wonder. "The back of the creature was spined with saw-tooth, triangular, leathery plates or fins that tapered up from a thick coupling on the body to sharp-edged points. *The body itself had the color and texture of green Jello over a deep brown background.* It was very real and literally awesome."

Then, as they watched, the creature submerged, only to resurface moments later to a height that revealed the slithery body between the humps. It was, without doubt, one long thick-bodied creature, the size of a small submarine. Eventually, it sank from sight. "The entire incident," Denise recalls, "from beginning to end, felt to me to go on for almost five minutes, but my husband, Bill, feels it was not quite that long in time."

If they disagree on the length of time of the sighting, it was the only aspect of the phenomenal experience that was not shared in common accord by all five people in the boat. To this day, they all attest, unequivocally, to having seen precisely the same thing.

Lynnette Nahirney, pointing to the spot in the center of Lake Okanagan where the creature was sighted.

Lynnette Nahirney, standing by one of many SIGHTING STATIONS that dot the shores of Lake Okanagan.

Photos courtesy of:
The Nahirney Family

The following are excerpts of letters written to the Author
Friday, April 19/91

Dear Mel,

Enclosed is the book 'Whalers No More' - see page 178.

This diagram of the Cadborosaurus (Caddy) is most representative of
what a young Ogopogo would look like. As a tadpole changes form,
this 'animal' would lose the fin tail and develop a dinosaur body, with
'humps' and the triangular 'plates' on the back.

The author is Wm. A. Hagelund, of Burnaby, B.C., and do call him
if you are interested in having this information in your book. . .

> *Denise Nahirney*
> *Museum Co-Ordinator,*
> *The B.C. Orchard Industry Museum*

May 5th, 1991

Dear Mel,

Thank you for your letter of April 24th, and your request to use the
Caddy info in 'Whalers No More' for your upcoming book, 'The
Ogopogo Affair'. . .

The sea creature reportedly found in a sperm whale landed at Naden
Harbour in 1936, and the tiny sea creature found by myself in Pirates
Cove in 1970, as described on pages 178 and 179 in Harbour
Publishing's (1987) Award winning book, 'Whalers No More' and
the pictures therein, are hereby offered to you. . .credits to be duly
published in your book, 'The Ogopogo Affair.'

> *Bill*
> *WM. A. Hagelund*
> *6719 Bryant Street*
> *Burnaby, B.C. V2E 1S7*

PAGES 178 and 179 of 'WHALERS NO MORE' BY WM. A. HAGELUND

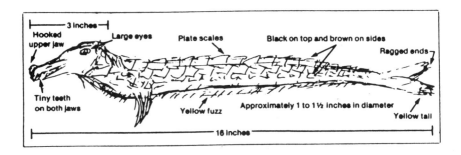

.... small, eel-like, sea creature swimming along with its head held completely out of the water, the undulation of this long, slender body causing portions of its spine to break the surface. My first thought that it was a sea snake was quickly discarded when, on drawing closer, I noticed the dark limpid eyes, large in proportion to the slender head which had given it a seal-like appearance when viewed from the front. When it turned away, a long, slightly hooked snout could be discerned.

As the evening's darkness made observation difficult, and the swiftness of the creature's progress warned that he could quickly disappear, I decided to attempt a capture and bring it aboard the sloop for closer examination. Reaching out with a small dip net as Gerry swung the stern of our dinghy into the path of the small vee of wavelets that were the only indication of the creature's position, I was pleased to find him twisting angrily in the net when I lifted it up.

Under the bright lights aboard the sloop, we examined our catch and found he was approximately sixteen inches long, and just over an inch in diameter. His lower jaw had a set of sharp tiny teeth, and his back was protected by plate-like scales, while his undersides were covered in a soft yellow fuzz. A pair of small, flipper-like feet protruded from his shoulder area, and a spade-shaped tail proved to be two tiny flipper-like fins that overlapped each other.

I felt the biological people at Departure Bay would be interested in this find, but without a radiophone to contact them, the next best thing was to sail up there in the morning. Agreeing on this, we filled a large plastic bucket with sea water and dumped our creature into it. We retired early, for I intended to leave at first light, but sleep would not come to me. Instead, I lay awake, acutely aware of the little creature trapped in our bucket. In the stillness of the anchorage I could hear the splashes made by his tail, and the scratching of his little teeth and flippers as he attempted to grasp the smooth surface of the bucket. Such exertion, I began to realize, could cause him to perish before morning.

My uneasiness grew until I finally climbed back on deck and shone my flashlight down into the bucket. He stopped swimming immediately, and faced the light as though it were an enemy, his mouth open slightly, the lips drawn back exposing his teeth, and the tufts of whiskers standing stiffly out from each side of his snout, while his large eyes reflected the glare of my flashlight. I felt a strong compassion for that little face staring up at me, so bravely awaiting its fate.

Just as strongly came the feeling that, if he was a rare creature as my limited knowledge led me to believe, then the miracle of his being in Pirates Cove at all should not be undone by my impulsive capture. He should be allowed to go free, to survive, if possible, and fulfil his purpose. If he were successful, we could possibly see more of his kind, not less. If he perished in my hands, he would only be a forgotten curiosity. I lowered the bucket over the side and watched him swim ....

Page one, Vancouver Province, October 16, 1937 --- Infant "Caddy" found in whale. The fisheries department's news bulletin today described a strange creature taken from the stomach of a Pacific Coast whale, tallying closely with descriptions of the elusive *Cadborosaurus* of Southern Vancouver Island waters, but much smaller, possibly an infant. Officials said it was surprising to find such a large creature in a whale's stomach, as the mammals feed usually on squid, octopus, and sometimes shrimp. Discovery of the infant mammal was reported in the Daily Province in July. It was found at Naden Harbour whaling station, and its exact species has never been determined.

Vancouver Province, same day, on page 31 --- Officials reading the report of the Naden Harbour Whaling Station were surprised to find in it this description of an animal taken from the stomach of a whale killed off Queen Charlotte Islands: "About 10 feet long, having a head similar to a large dog, animal-like vertebrae and having a tail resembling a single blade of gill bone as found in whale's jaws."

AUTHOR'S NOTE:

Could the above excerpt of pages 178 and 179 of Wm. A. Hagelund's award-winning book "Whalers No More," so meticulously told in every detail, have any relevance to the distant origins of our own OGOPOGO? When we refer back to Denise Nahirney's description of the creature she and her family encountered in the waters of Lake Okanagan in September, 1988, and compare her observations with those of Mr. Hagelund's, one can only speculate, and wonder.

ONE FINAL 'SIGHTING' BY MOONLIGHT

Margaret Girou's sketch of what she saw

IN HER OWN WORDS:

My husband, Ernie Girou, is a retired big game guide, originally from Fernie, B.C. We came to Kelowna in 1964.

In the Fall of 1989, my husband and I, and our two dogs, were camped for two weeks in our Motorhome at Bear Creek Provincial Park, on the western shore of Lake Okanagan.

At about 9 pm on the night of September 15th, there was a full moon and a clear sky, and we decided to walk our dogs around the island where the boats are docked near the mouth of Bear Creek. I happened to look back and I sighted this 'creature' silhouetted in the moonlight. It was slithering through the water like a snake about fifty yards off shore. We were both stunned by what we were seeing.

As my husband put it: "It had a round head like a football and about two to three feet of the head and body stuck up out of the water. It was at least fifteen feet long with the pointed tail also sticking up out of the water."

It was swimming swiftly and gracefully to our left, with no splashing of any kind. We watched it for about ten minutes before it dove down and disappeared, but it came up again, swimming in the opposite direction, then it disappeared for the second time. We continued to watch for some time but it did not reappear.

Our family wanted us to report the sighting but we held back for quite a while. It was the report that told of Ogopogo being a beaver or an otter, that finally got us 'burned up' enough to go to the media.

As Ernie says, "I've seen a lot of animals swimming in the wilds and what we saw that night was definitely not a beaver or an otter. Beavers don't swim like that. It was jutting too far out of the water to be a beaver. And then there's the tail. A beaver's tail is flat, not like the pointed tail we saw that night."

Ernie says, "I've never believed in Ogopogo, but there's *something* out there."

That's what I think now, too.

This photograph was taken from the mouth of Bear Creek where the Girou's were camped. Ogopogo was spotted about fifty yards from shore.

Margaret and Ernie Girou at their home in Kelowna. Ernie is a retired big game guide. Not a man to be easily fooled.

65

MEL D. AMES

EPILOGUE

There are believers and there are those who scoff. There are those who have seen Ogopogo, or believe they have, and there are those who never have and never will. But seeing *is* believing, after all, and who are we to question those who excitedly articulate on one of the most memorable moments of their lives?

I have been asked if I, personally, believe that Ogopogo actually exists. *That*, I reply, is a little like asking if I believe in ghosts. I have never seen a ghost, nor have I seen Ogopogo, so I tend to approach both phenomena with cautious ambivalence. That is not to say they do, or do not exist. It simply takes us back to the old adage, 'seeing is believing', and if we can persuade ourselves to accept the objectivity of those who *have* had the experience, it becomes incumbent on the rest of us, I should think, to offer them some modicum of credibility, if not outright acceptance.

I defy anyone to listen firsthand to Denise Nahirney as she tells of her 'sighting' of the lake creature, and come away unmoved. The same applies, of course, to those others who have held the Holy Grail, so to speak, where no amount of rationalization is able to stir them from their certainty. And that is as it should be.

Peter Sellers, editor of the Cold Blood Anthologies currently in publication by Mosaic Press, spoke to me by telephone as I was putting this book together. He knew of the book, of course, and he knew (even from as far away as Toronto) of the Ogopogo legend. ''I hope the creature is never captured,'' he stated sagely, ''because such an event could destroy, or certainly compromise, the lake monster's magnificent mystique that has already endured the ravages of time for over a century.''

I, for one, sincerely hope that Peter's words become a self-fulfilling prophecy, don't you?

Historic Packing House Label
Courtesy of:
B.C. Orchard Industry Museum